Beast Quest®

GoroG
THE FIERY FIEND

BY ADAM BLADE

ORCHARD

With special thanks to Tabitha Jones

To Jack Staniforth

www.beastquest.co.uk

ORCHARD BOOKS

First published in Great Britain in 2021 by The Watts Publishing Group

1 3 5 7 9 10 8 6 4 2

Text © Beast Quest Limited 2021
Cover and inside illustrations by Steve Sims
© Beast Quest Limited 2021

Beast Quest is a registered trademark of Beast Quest Limited
Series created by Beast Quest Limited, London

A CIP catalogue record for this book is available from the British Library.

ISBN 978 1 40836 526 7

Printed in Great Britain

The paper and board used in this book are made from wood from responsible sources

Orchard Books
An imprint of Hachette Children's Group
Part of The Watts Publishing Group Limited
Carmelite House, 50 Victoria Embankment, London EC4Y 0DZ

An Hachette UK Company
www.hachette.co.uk
www.hachettechildrens.co.uk

Welcome to the world of Beast Quest!

Tom was once an ordinary village boy, until he travelled to the City, met King Hugo and discovered his destiny. Now he is the Master of the Beasts, sworn to defend Avantia and its people against Evil. Tom draws on the might of the magical Golden Armour, and is protected by powerful tokens granted to him by the Good Beasts of Avantia. Together with his loyal companion Elenna, Tom is always ready to visit new lands and tackle the enemies of the realm.

While there's blood in his veins, Tom will never give up the Quest...

There are special gold coins to collect in this book. You will earn one coin for every chapter you read.

Find out what to do with your coins at the end of the book.

CONTENTS

For a time, I was the most powerful Master of the Beasts who ever walked this land. A royal prince. A courageous hero. People chanted my name.

But at the peak of my fame, it was taken from me by cowards.

For almost three centuries my spirit has wandered the realms. In ghostly form, I have searched for the one magical token that will bring me back.

And now I have found it, Avantia will pay for her treachery.

Only a fool would stand in my path.

Karadin

THE BURIED HAND

The clang of steel on steel jerked Tom from his sleep, setting his pulse thudding. He sat up, reaching for his sword. *Is the palace under attack?* But then he heard a cheerful shout from outside, followed by a laugh, and he remembered: the noise was no battle. Captain Harkman's workmen were fixing the palace drainage system. Tom lay back down with a groan, pulling his warm bedclothes tighter, trying to find sleep again, but another loud bang was followed by the rhythmic ringing of a pickaxe on stone.

He sighed. *This is hopeless!*

He rubbed his eyes and swung his legs out of bed. It was barely dawn and thin silvery light filtered through the gap in the shutters. Setting his feet on the chilly flagstones, Tom shrugged his tunic over his head, yanked on his boots then left his room. *I may as well get breakfast!*

Elenna was already ahead of him, making her own way down to the kitchens. "Good morning!" Tom called. As his friend turned, he had to stifle a grin. Scowling fiercely and with her short hair sticking up in messy tufts, she looked even grumpier about being up than him.

"Good?" Elenna grumbled. "I don't see what's good about it. How long does it take to fix a few pipes? And I still don't understand why work has to start so early! Every. Single. Day."

Tom chuckled. "After all the places we've slept on our Quests you're bothered by a bit of noise? Although, I have to admit, there's something about being woken at the crack of dawn when you're tucked up in a feather bed that does grate a little." He shrugged. "But the sooner they start, the sooner they'll finish, I suppose."

"Well, it can't be soon enough for me!" Elenna replied, pushing open the door to the kitchens. A warm burst of air engulfed Tom, along with the smell of bacon frying. His stomach growled in anticipation and he felt instantly more cheerful. But before he could enter, a sharp, fearful cry from outside pulled him up short.

"Fire!" another voice yelled from the courtyard.

Elenna turned to Tom with a sigh.

"Sounds like breakfast will have to wait," she said.

Tom nodded. "We'd better find out what's going on!"

They hurried together through the palace and headed out into the chilly dawn to see King Hugo already striding across the courtyard towards the stable block. Brownish smoke coiled upwards from the worksite near the stables where the drainage was being repaired. Tom felt a jolt of worry for the horses and quickened his step.

"Get back!" Harkman cried, urgently shooing three burly workmen away from a jagged trench in the ground. The workmen gaped at the hole, their shovels and pickaxes hanging limply in their hands as more smoke billowed up.

"What's going on?" King Hugo asked, reaching the captain and his men at the same time as Tom and Elenna did.

Harkman gestured to the trench. "In there!" he said. "Some kind of smoke. But there're no flames. And it stinks!"

Elenna clapped a hand over her nose just as Tom got a whiff of the most revolting stench he'd ever smelled. A mix of burned hair, rotten eggs and sewage.

"Move away!" Harkman told his men again. Tom and Elenna stepped past them to the edge of the trench and peered down through the smoke, which spiralled slowly upwards. The smell was so bad it made Tom's head swim.

"What's that?" Elenna said, pointing downwards. Right in the bottom of the hole, partly covered by dirt, Tom spotted a rectangular metal object, about the length of his forearm, and covered in rust. A few final wisps of smoke cleared, and Tom saw it was some kind of box.

"Careful," he cried, as Harkman leapt down to retrieve it.

The captain quickly brushed away loose soil and prised the container free. "It's just an old box," he said, climbing back out of the hole and holding the object where everyone could see it. "There are some markings on the top, though." The metalwork was so corroded it was hard to make out the etchings, but, peering closely, Tom saw twin swords, crossed above the hilt.

"That looks almost like a coat of arms," King Hugo said, rubbing at his beard. "But not one I recognise."

Harkman gave the lid a tug. "It's rusted shut," he said.

"What's going on?" Daltec asked, arriving at the worksite with his cloak pulled crookedly over his nightgown. His face creased. 'What's that dreadful smell?'

Harkman held up the box. "It came from the hole where we found this," he said. "But it won't open."

Daltec took the box, frowning at the rusted seam along its edge. "It may be an enchantment of some sort," he said. "There might be more fumes, so we should open it out here in the fresh air. Everyone stand back."

Tom shuffled a few paces away from the young wizard, expecting him to use some kind of spell. But

Daltec stooped to take a chisel from a nearby pile of tools and worked it under the lid. The box opened stiffly, with a grating sound.

Daltec gasped, almost dropping the box.

"What is it?" Tom asked, leaning in closer for a better view.

A breath of cold, dank air hit him. If felt as if he'd stepped into a mouldy old cellar. Or a crypt. The box was lined with

moth-eaten velvet, and nestled inside, yellowed with age, was a single skeleton hand.

BODY OF SHADOW

Elenna took a step back, grimacing.
"Ugh! How horrible!" she said,
breaking the silence as everyone
stared at the gruesome object.
"Where's the rest of the skeleton?
And who buries a severed hand on
its own?"

Tom noticed a tarnished ring on
the hand's knobbly index finger.

Looking more closely, he saw that it was worked in the shape of a snake eating its own tail, with a colourless gem for an eye. The dull gleam of the gem filled him with a cold, creeping dread he couldn't explain. "Someone who hoped it would never be found, I suppose," he said.

King Hugo shook himself and cleared his throat, as if waking from a bad dream. Then he tugged at his beard, frowning. Tom had rarely seen the king look so uncertain. "Since it's on palace grounds, we must assume it belonged to someone with royal blood," Hugo said. "Regardless, we should rebury it properly. Ideally, with the rest of whoever it belonged to. Do you have any idea who it could be?" he asked Daltec.

"I don't," Daltec said, frowning down at the hand. "They must have died long ago. I'll have to check the palace records."

"Good idea!" Hugo said. "I will leave it with you until we can arrange a suitable burial." The king turned to Captain Harkman. "I think it would be prudent to finish work here as quickly as possible. And if any other...*artefacts* are discovered, please let me know at once."

"Of course," Harkman said. Then he turned to address his men. "You heard the king! Back to work!"

Tom saw Hugo hesitate before setting off towards the palace, shaking his head as he went. He couldn't blame the king for feeling uneasy. Tom had seen plenty of skeletons on his Quests, but even that hadn't prepared him for the shock of uncovering a single severed hand, and so close to home. He shuddered.

As Daltec started to close the box, Tom caught a hint of movement from inside, as if the bony index finger had flexed.

"Wait!" Tom told Daltec, his heart thumping hard. "It moved!"

Daltec chuckled nervously, and opened the box fully again. Everyone watched the hand closely.

It lay completely still, nestled in velvet. The only faint stirring was of the sunlight, glinting on the gemstone in the ring. "I thought... the finger twitched," Tom said, realising suddenly how foolish he sounded. *Like a frightened child.*

"Just a trick of the light, surely!" Harkman said, heartily. "You had me worried for a moment there, Tom!"

"Or it could be the effect of those fumes!" Elenna added, putting a hand on Tom's shoulder. "I still feel a bit giddy from the smell."

The sun had risen fully and the courtyard was filled with servants chatting as they fetched water and fed livestock. Looking at the hand now, bathed in light and perfectly still, Tom nodded. "Yes...that must be it," he said.

Tom did his best to put the incident from his mind. But during the rest of the day, while he was oiling Storm's saddle, or just walking down a corridor, the sudden image of that bony finger bending, as if beckoning...alive...kept flashing through his mind.

Once night had fallen and the fire in Tom's room had burned low, he found himself tossing and turning in bed despite his early start. His lids were heavy with exhaustion, but every time he shut his eyes, the hand was there, waiting in the darkness. Daltec had spent most of the day in the library but, though he had searched every tome, he could shed no light on the severed hand or the ring it wore. He had found no mention of the crossed-swords motif, either.

Why would someone bury a hand? Tom wondered. *And how can there be no record? It's just so strange...*

He rolled over and stared at the wall. Suddenly a hoarse, rasping voice, almost too faint to hear, hissed in his ear: "*Where is it?*"

Tom sat bolt upright, his skin fizzing with shock. He stared into the gloom, searching every shadow, but the room was empty. The sound didn't come again. *Maybe I was dreaming after all?* His pulse began to slow, but then a raw, panicked cry, this time familiar and further away, tore through the night. *Daltec!* Tom realised. He sprang from his bed.

"Help!"

The wizard's muffled voice sounded terrified. Grabbing his sword and shield, Tom raced from his chamber, running as fast as he could towards Daltec's tower. He took the stairs to Daltec's room three at a time.

When he reached the door, he wrenched the handle, but it

wouldn't budge. And now all Tom could hear from inside were strangled whimpers.

"Daltec!" Tom shouted. "I'm coming!" Calling on the strength of his golden breastplate, Tom braced himself, then threw his full weight against the door. *THUD!* The door shuddered. Again Tom smashed his shoulder into the wood, ignoring the pain. Finally, on the third strike, it burst open. Tom tumbled inside

to see Daltec crouching on the floor, clawing weakly at the edge of his desk. His bloodshot eyes were wide with terror, and the skeleton hand was clamped hard over his nose and mouth, smothering him. In the dim firelight, Tom made out more...a shadowy arm, the hint of a muscular shoulder and draping cloak. *A shadow figure!*

And it was trying to kill his friend.

1

3

THE MIDNIGHT COUNCIL

"Get off him!" Tom roared, brandishing his sword. With a hiss, the shadow figure leapt away, releasing Daltec. The wizard slumped to the ground, gasping for air as the dark stranger turned towards Tom. Tom took in the spectre's cavernous cheeks and

scowl of hatred; the dark, hollow pits of its eyes. The figure's lips curled into a disdainful smile.

"You are rather young to be a Master of the Beasts," it said, in a rasping whisper that sent an icy finger down Tom's spine. It was the same voice he had heard in his room. Tom lunged, but with inhuman speed, the shadow man dived towards the tower's balcony window and leapt through, out into the night. Tom raced to the window and looked after the figure, but the courtyard far below was shrouded in darkness and he couldn't see any sign of movement.

He turned back to the room, and found Daltec getting unsteadily to his feet. "Are you all right?" Tom asked his friend.

Daltec was shaking, his face a pale mask of horror, but he nodded. "Thanks to you," he croaked.

"Good," Tom said. "I'll be back." He vaulted up on to the edge of the balcony and leapt. Cool air rushed up to meet him as he plummeted. Raising his shield, Tom called on the power of Arcta's eagle feather. Instantly it slowed his fall. Tom swooped towards the flagstones and landed in a crouch. Peering into the shadows, he searched the courtyard. It was utterly still and silent.

Where is he?

Suddenly, an eerie rattling whinny echoed from the darkness. Tom spun to see a mighty stallion galloping towards him, black as the night but with the courtyard clearly visible through its form. The shadow man sat astride the horse, his skeleton hand clamped tight about the reins and his lips twisted into a rictus of hatred.

Tom lifted his sword and sank into a fighting stance. As the shadow horse sped closer, Tom felt again the chilly breath of the grave envelop him. He smelled the mouldy, dusty stench of death.

The horse closed on him. Looking up into the dead, empty eyes of its rider, Tom stepped aside and

swung his sword straight for the shadow man's chest. His blade met no resistance, and Tom staggered forwards as the stallion thundered past, buffeting him with a gust of dank, putrid-smelling wind.

How can I fight a shadow?! Teeth gritted in frustration, Tom swung around and raced after the horse as it careened towards the portcullis. A single guard manned the gate. Tom saw the man's eyes open wide with terror as the shadow horse and its rider neared. The steed wasn't slowing. If anything, it galloped harder, its dark rider leaning forwards in the saddle, craning low over the horse's neck. As it reached the barred gate, the horse's step didn't falter. Its muscles bunched and it leapt right through the solid metal and wood, leaving only a few wisps of shadow in its wake.

"Raise the portcullis!" Tom roared as he drew near to the startled guard. The man started turning the winch clumsily with shaking hands. Elbowing him aside, Tom took the guard's place and raised the gate enough to slip under, but the dark landscape was empty. The moon slid from behind a cloud at that same moment, bathing the road ahead in silver light. But there was no sign of anything moving – alive or dead.

A short time later, Tom sat at the table in King Hugo's chamber, waiting for His Majesty's midnight council to begin. A fire burned in the grate and candles lit the room, but Tom found himself glancing into the shadows half expecting to see a ghostly figure, or a pale bony hand. Opposite Tom, seated between the king and the former wizard, Aduro, Daltec hugged his cloak tightly about himself as if he couldn't get warm. He looked pale and haunted, with deep scratch marks around his nose and mouth. Tom shuddered, thinking of how close he'd come to losing his friend.

At Tom's side, Elenna sat quiet and grave, and beside her was Harkman, hunched, his hands clasped in front of him. Thankfully, Queen Aroha and baby Thomas were both safely away in Tangala, far from any harm.

Tom frowned as he gazed at the metal box in the centre of the table.

Apart from the crossed swords, it was unadorned. Just a rusty metal box. But it held so much mystery.

"Aduro, have you been able to find out anything that would explain this... dreadful business?" Hugo gestured vaguely toward the box, and then to Daltec. The king looked almost as haunted as the young wizard, his brows knitted together and his face lined with worry.

Aduro shook his head. "Very little," he said. "I have learned that the sigil of the crossed swords was used for a short while by King Mandor."

Hugo's frown deepened at the name. "King Mandor ruled centuries ago. Do you mean to tell me that box has been in the ground all this time?"

Tom had never heard the name and from Elenna's face, he guessed she hadn't either.

Aduro sighed heavily. "Perhaps. The records from his time are very sparse, I am afraid. He was an unhappy man, by all accounts. One of the few things I could find out from the *Chronicles of Avantia* was that he never produced an heir."

All the candles guttered suddenly and went out, pitching the table into darkness. Tom heard a deep, unearthly voice echo around the chamber. "The records are false."

Everyone jumped and Tom leapt up, turning to see a shimmering grey figure by the door – transparent and almost too dim to see in the firelight, but muscular, and wearing the armour of a knight. Tom's hand went to his sword.

The figure bowed its head in greeting. "You will not need a weapon, friends," said the man, in a deep calm voice.

"How did you get in here?" Harkman

demanded.

"Walls and locked doors mean nothing to one from the Realm of Ghosts," said the man. "I am Mandor's son, Prince Loris. And I bring bad tidings."

Tom let his sword slide back into its sheath.

Aduro leaned forwards, his drawn brows deeply shadowing his eyes. "Mandor had a son?" he said.

"Two," said Loris. "I fear you have already met my brother, Karadin."

From his dark tone, Tom guessed he meant the phantom who'd almost killed Daltec.

"I can't say it was a pleasure," said the young wizard.

"How extraordinary!" King Hugo said, blinking into the darkness.

Loris's translucent face was youthful and unlined, but he somehow looked old and tired at the same time. And terribly sad.

"I spent my whole life in Karadin's shadow. He was the cruellest, most power-hungry man in all of Avantia's history. Now that you have uncovered his buried hand, he has returned. And he will stop at nothing to take Avantia's throne."

PRINCE LORIS

Loris's glimmering apparition stepped further into the room and Tom saw his eyes clearly for the first time: large and pale, filled with anguish. "You have to stop Karadin, before he draws more power to himself," Loris said, balling his fists. "Before it is too late!"

Moved by the ghost's sorrow

and determination, Tom bowed. "While there is blood in my veins, I will fight to stop him!" he told the spectre. "Tell us everything you can."

Loris nodded. "Our tale is not a happy one, my brother's and mine, but it is short."

Tom settled himself to listen, and while the rest of the council waited in tense silence, Loris began...

"Almost three hundred years ago, my father, King Mandor, ruled Avantia. At that time, many terrible Beasts roamed the kingdom, laying waste to villages and towns. My father decided that Karadin and I would share the role of Master of the Beasts. My brother was a fearless man, but also ruthless and vain. He had never been kind to me, but I trusted him to treat me as a brother should, so we left the palace together, in search of Beasts. Before long, we came upon a village that was being terrorised by Gargantua the Silent Assassin.

Together, my brother and I subdued the Beast. But when Karadin was about to strike the killing blow,

Gargantua offered him a deal. *Kill Loris instead of me, and I will make you the most powerful man ever to live.* Without hesitation, my brother turned his sword on me.

"Unwilling to fight my own kin, I tried to retreat, but I was slain – stabbed in the back." Loris smiled bitterly at the memory. "I wish there had been the sweet release of a natural death, but instead, I had to watch and endure what followed while in this ghostly form. My brother returned to our father, and told him that I had died valiantly, in battle. Father mourned me.

"But what Father did not know was that Gargantua had taken the form of a magical ring, which Karadin now wore on his finger. Every time my brother defeated a Beast, the ring absorbed its essence, giving him power over the spirit of each vanquished creature. So, as Gargantua had promised, Karadin became stronger and stronger. But, while the people hailed Karadin as a hero, my father saw how he had delighted in his new role, and had never seemed to mourn me, his brother. The king grew suspicious.

"Finally, my father sent troops to the site of our first battle. My body was discovered; slain not by a Beast as my brother had said,

but with a sword. Father ordered
his wizard to spy on Karadin, and
the secret of the ring was soon
discovered. When confronted,
Karadin refused to submit, and in
the struggle that followed his hand
was severed, along with the ring."
Loris gestured towards the empty
box on the table. "So ashamed
was he of his error of judgement,
my father banished Karadin, and
erased all record of both his sons
from history. Karadin has hunted
for his hand ever since, while I have
been forced to walk the shadows,
unable to live, or to truly die." Loris's
shoulders drooped. "I told you...not a
happy story."

By the time Prince Loris had finished relaying the sorry tale, the fire had burned to embers. Pink streaks showed in the sky outside, and the first birds were hailing the dawn.

King Hugo shook his head, frowning. "To think that such a terrible secret lies in Avantia's royal lineage. It's hard to fathom how such a dark tale can have been kept from us!"

"I assure you, it is true!" Loris cried, wringing his hands, his pale eyes beseeching Tom.

"We believe you," Tom told

the ghost. "But how can we find Karadin?"

"Now he has his ring back, he will be after Avantia's throne," Loris said. "To take it, he will need an army. I believe he will return to the domain of each Beast he defeated, in order to resurrect them, under his own control."

Tom nodded gravely. "Where do you think he will go first?" he asked the ghost.

"I followed him some way to gauge his direction," Loris said. "He was heading west, towards the Forest of Fear. There he will unleash Gorog, a huge varkule-Beast that he defeated long ago."

Tom's gut twisted with dread. He had battled varkules before. Long extinct and brought back only by evil magic, they were brutish, bloodthirsty creatures – hard enough to defeat in their natural form. A varkule-*Beast* would be a terrible foe indeed.

"Maybe we can head Karadin off, and stop him raising Gorog?" Elenna asked.

"I think we have to try," Tom said. "Which means we should leave right away."

After gathering the few provisions they would need for the

journey, Tom and Elenna left for the Forest of Fear. They rode together on Storm, with Silver, Elenna's wolf, scouting ahead. It had been a long while since both animals had accompanied them on a Quest and each time Tom spotted Silver's grey form in the distance, he felt thankful. Though the old wolf's muzzle was tinged with white, his teeth were as sharp as ever, and so were his senses. Nothing would creep up on them in the dense undergrowth of the Forest of Fear without Silver raising the alarm.

They rode hard, with few breaks, and by mid-afternoon the first towering firs of the forest's treeline loomed above them.

Silver let out a low growl as he entered the forest, and Storm shook his head, snorting uneasily. As they passed from the bright afternoon and beneath the tree canopy, it was as if all colour and light had been sapped from the world, leaving it shadowy and cold. Tall conifers blocked out the sun, and thorny bushes pressed in on either side, snagging Tom's clothes and scratching his skin as Storm trotted onwards. Sitting behind him in the saddle, Elenna shivered.

"This has to be one of my least favourite places," she said. Tom could tell her words were meant to be light, but they came out too loud in the dead air. He scanned the gloomy shadows, feeling the electric tingle of unfriendly eyes, watching, waiting... They pressed on, the forest silent around them except for Storm's steady hoofbeats, muffled by fallen pine needles.

The further they travelled, the darker it became, until the only sign of Silver stalking ahead was the amber glow of his eyes when he glanced back to check they were following. The ground became boggy, forcing Storm to slow. Mud, green with slime, popped and squelched beneath his hooves, sending up bursts of foul-smelling fumes.

Skirting around a dense, tangled thicket with thorns as long as Tom's hand, they found Silver waiting for them at the bank of a stagnant pool. The wolf let out an anxious whine as Tom pulled Storm to a halt. The water was a phosphorescent green, and a stench like rotten eggs was almost

 overpowering, catching in Tom's throat and making his eyes sting. Tom heard a faint plop, followed by a splash; scanning the water, he thought he could see something lithe and dark, moving... Storm tossed his head and backed away.

"It's all right, boy," Tom said, steadying the horse, although the sight of the pool filled him with dread. Who knew what foul creatures dwelled beneath the surface?

"Tom, look at the trees," Elenna said, pointing at the trunks closest to the pool. Tom saw that all were rotten and black. Some had been eaten almost through, burned by the acidic water. He and Elenna slid from Storm's saddle and gingerly skirted around the pool, leading Storm by the reins.

With the pond behind them, they made their way among twisted, leafless trees festooned with hairy vines. Storm's flanks twitched uneasily as Tom led him between rotting ferns and clumps of reddish fungi. A tendril of vine brushed Tom's neck, and he shuddered and shook it off. It felt exactly like a cold, clammy hand. Suddenly, Silver howled up ahead, high and panicked. Storm reared at the sound, tearing free of Tom's grip.

Tom tried to grab his horse's reins, but Silver howled again, and Storm bucked and whinnied, his huge hooves wheeling and his eyes rolling.

"Whoa!" Tom said. But as the stallion brought his hooves crashing down, he broke into a run, plunging through the thick vegetation and away.

"Silver!" Elenna called into the forest. "Come!" But only silence greeted her. Even Storm's hoofbeats had faded away.

"Something's spooked the animals," Tom said, peering into the dank vegetation. "We'd better get after them." He set off, scanning the way ahead for any sign of Storm or Silver, but all he could make out was a thin patch of silvery mist between two trees – just a strange trick of the light, perhaps. *Whoa!* Tom stopped abruptly. It wasn't mist. It was Loris! The ghost was little more than a milky shadow, and Tom had almost walked right through him. Stepping back and squinting, Tom made out the dead prince more clearly, pointing into the deep undergrowth ahead.

"Look!" Loris said, just as a light

appeared among the trees. Not the welcome light of a dwelling, or the sun peeking through leaves, but a pale and sickly glow, getting steadily brighter by the moment.

Tom grabbed Elenna's arm, just as a smell hit him – decay and death, ashes and rot. His skin crawled and he almost retched. Something was there, just ahead of them. Something evil.

5

BATTLE OF THE BROTHERS

Tom and Elenna crept silently through the damp, slimy foliage, darting from tree to tree so as not to be seen. The light ahead brightened until it made Tom wince. Shielding his eyes from the glare, he ducked through a tangle of vines and out into a clearing. He shrank back

instantly, putting up a hand to stop
Elenna.

At the centre of the muddy space
stood a cloaked figure with a
skeletal hand raised aloft. *Karadin!*
White light streamed from the ring
on Karadin's finger, making his
shadow form appear blacker than
ever. He was taller and broader than
his brother, with a sharp-featured,
clean-shaven face, while his eyes
were like holes of darkness; empty,
bottomless pits.

As Tom watched, Karadin lowered
his arm, pointing his ringed finger
towards the ground. The pulsing,
platinum light hit the earth, and
seemed to pierce deep into it, like

a searing
flame or a
blade. All
around the
point where
it struck,
the ground
started to
crack and
drop away,
forming a
pit.

"You are too late!" Loris cried,
appearing suddenly at Tom's elbow.
"I have to stop this!"

The ghost prince darted into the
clearing. The widening crater almost
filled it now, and was lined with

crackling veins of light.

"Stop!" Loris commanded his brother. The shadow man's eyes snapped up to meet those of the younger ghost, and his face twisted into a sneer of contempt.

"You..." Karadin hissed. "I destroyed you once. I can do it again!" Karadin lunged at his brother, grabbing for the spectre's throat with his skeleton hand. Loris ducked just in time, then leapt, slamming a fist into Karadin's jaw. Karadin stumbled back with a growl of fury, before rounding on his brother once more and aiming a jab at his throat.

The two ghostly figures skirted

around the edge of the growing crater, throwing fierce punches and kicks.

Elenna took out an arrow and notched it in a heartbeat. She let the shaft fly, right towards Karadin's head, but it flew straight through.

"Karadin's made of shadow," Tom said. "The only bit of him that we can touch is his hand. And anyway, I think we've got more to worry about." Tom pointed into the crater. The edge was only paces away now and the light-veined earth at the bottom was rising and falling slowly.

"It's like it's...breathing," Elenna said.

Tom's mouth was dry as he watched the glowing earth stretch and shrink. It was strangely hypnotic. A scream from Loris cut Tom off. Looking up, he blinked hard, trying to work out what he was seeing. Karadin was towering over his brother, who was on his knees. One of Karadin's hands – the bone one – was clamped around Loris's throat, while the other had become a mass of coiling, shadowy tendrils which were forcing their way into Loris's mouth. The younger ghost's body swelled and deformed, warping horribly like wet clay being stretched. His eyes bulged as he writhed and squirmed.

Karadin's invading Loris's body – possessing him! Tom realised. Sick with horror, he brandished his sword, ready to leap to Loris's aid… *But how? Karadin's a ghost. Maybe if I aim for his hand?* But before Tom could round the gaping pit in front of him, Loris let out a gargled cry and hurled his fist hard into his brother's gut.

Karadin reeled back with a howl of pain and fury, while Loris, returning to his normal shape, staggered up.

"I'm coming, Loris!" Tom told the ghost. "I'll fight with you to the end!" But Karadin had unbent too, and was making a horrible choking sound. No... Not choking. He was *laughing*.

"You've already lost!" Karadin hissed. Tom lowered his eyes to the wide pit in the ground, and swallowed hard. A huge mound of dark, matted fur was rising up, uncoiling, revealing a muzzle crammed with curved fangs and, above that, a pair of huge, glowing red eyes.

Elenna grabbed Tom's arm and yanked him back.

"Gorog's awake!" she cried.

THE RISE OF GOROG

Before Tom could raise his sword again, Gorog bounded from the pit on all fours. The Beast lowered his massive head, drool dripping from his fangs, and barrelled straight into Tom and Elenna. The varkule-Beast's shoulder caught Tom square in the chest, knocking the air from his lungs and flinging him backwards. He rolled over and over, slammed into a tree and came to a stop, gasping and dizzy. He pulled himself up to see Elenna rising slowly, rubbing her shoulder. Ahead of them, Gorog had turned and was staggering around the huge pit towards Karadin. The shadow man was still cackling with triumph, while Loris had vanished.

With an angry snort, the Beast shook his vast, shaggy head, then lifted his snout and howled. The terrible sound rose and fell like a full pack of wolves baying at the moon, and was so loud Tom had to clamp his hands over his ears.

Even crouched, the Beast was as tall
as a horse and far broader across
the haunches. Vast muscles bulged
beneath Gorog's tangled pelt, and
each huge foot bore black claws
that curved to points. At last, the

Beast fell quiet and lowered his head, pawing the ground as if about to charge Karadin. Elenna had an arrow aimed and ready, but with the Beast turned on their enemy, she didn't fire.

As Gorog approached, the shadow man lifted his skeleton hand and smiled. The ring on his finger started to pulse with light once more. The Beast froze, as if transfixed, staring at the ring. Slowly, Karadin moved his arm in an arc, his ringed finger sending out a beam of light that came to rest on Tom and Elenna. Gorog turned, his gaze following the beam, until he locked eyes with Tom.

Tom sank into a crouch, his sword lifted before him as the Beast let out a menacing growl. The sound rumbled around the clearing and Gorog's red eyes blazed brighter, like the coals at the heart of a fire. Tom stared into their depths, unblinking, his mind suddenly blank...

Tom tried to focus, but a terrible, paralysing fear gripped hold of him. All he could think of were the smouldering eyes. So red... So hot. Sweat broke out on his brow. His throat felt parched and his vision began to swim. It was as if he could feel the blazing orbs burning into his soul. And there was a smell too, of searing flesh. All at once, he realised the stench was coming from his own hands, gripped about the hilt of his sword. The blade was glowing the same deep, furnace red as the Beast's eyes. With a yelp, Tom thrust his blade into its scabbard and let go of the hilt, shaking his blistered hands in agony. His forearms were cramping with pain.

"The Beast..." he croaked to Elenna. "His eyes heated my sword!"

"Yes," Loris said, appearing suddenly at Tom's elbow. "Gorog's gaze will heat anything it rests on. Even—"

Whumpf! The dry needles at Tom's feet erupted into a blaze of flames as Gorog gazed at them. Tom and

Elenna
stumbled
back, but
the Beast's
deadly
stare
followed
them,
igniting
more leaf

litter which popped and crackled,
flames licking high.

"Run!" Elenna cried. Tom turned
and fled from the inferno raging
behind him. He could feel the
intense heat on his back as he
pounded through the trees, and
he could hear Karadin's booming

laughter. Glancing back, he saw the fire engulf a thorn bush. Branches exploded, spitting embers, catching more shrubs on either side. Tom ducked sideways but the flames followed him, then overtook him. Everywhere he looked the forest floor blazed, and thick, choking smoke billowed up.

"We have to climb!" Tom told Elenna as she stumbled at his side, her eyes filled with terror. He leapt for the nearest trunk, and started to shin up it. Elenna scrambled up behind him as the fire raged higher, catching ferns and making the thorn bushes writhe like snakes.

Tom reached for a branch, hauled

himself up and kept going, higher and higher. Black smoke swirled all around him and, when he looked down, he saw the base of the tree engulfed in flames. He glanced back to see Gorog following them, turning his massive head from side to side as he went, setting more trunks alight. Tom's eyes smarted and his throat and lungs burned. He could barely catch his breath.

"Keep going!" he wheezed to Elenna. Climbing out on a high, wide branch, Tom got to his feet and made a leap for the next tree. Elenna jumped too. But the trunk was already smouldering. Right behind them, Gorog let out a triumphant howl as Tom and Elenna leapt again. *We can't keep running!* Tom thought. *We have to fight.* But when he glanced down, all he could see was thick black smoke and deadly flames. He felt sick and dizzy from the heat, and his eyes streamed.

There was nothing he could do but keep going and risk passing out from the fumes or burning to death.

RAMPAGE OF THE VARKULE

Tom's head swam as he and Elenna scrambled from branch to branch and from tree to tree, the smoke thickening all around them until he could hardly see where to put his hands. Every touch of bark against his singed palms sent new blades of agony through him. He had to clamp

his teeth shut to keep from crying out. Tom made a grab for a bough just above, but in the spinning darkness, missed his grip. His stomach flipped as he fell, scrabbling in the air for a handhold.

"Oof!" He smashed into a lower branch and threw his arms around it. But where his skin touched wood, a terrible searing pain erupted, and through the smoke he could see

licking red and orange flames. The
branch was on fire! Panic clutching
hold of him, Tom found a foothold
and scrambled up, reaching high,
searching in the chaos of burning
leaves and twigs for a handhold.
Finding a narrow, solid branch, he
heaved himself upwards, clamped a
forearm over it and pulled the rest of
his body on to the bough. He shook
his hands, trying to ease the pain of
his burns. A hot wind gusted through
the canopy, and for a heartbeat, Tom
was clear of the smoke. He felt a
terrific jolting thud, and the tree
shuddered. Glancing down, he
caught a glimpse of Gorog ramming
his head into the trunk again with a

mighty *boom!* Tom scanned the way ahead before smoke filled his view, and saw something that gave him a flicker of hope. It was the pool that he and Elenna had passed earlier. *Elenna?* Tom's heart leapt and he looked about frantically, trying to think when he'd last seen her. But the smoke thickened again, blocking his view. The tree gave another wild shudder, and with a sickening crack, started to list. *Gorog's knocking it down!*

Bracing himself against the pain, Tom gripped a branch above once more and scrambled higher, up to the top of the tree where the trunk was narrow, but he still couldn't see

through the smoke. With a mighty
thud that jolted his bones, the tree
listed further, sloping steeply. Tom
suddenly made out the shadowy
form of another tree, just in reach.
He kicked off, made a grab for a
branch, then shimmied along it.
When he reached the thick wood near
the trunk, he saw Elenna. She was
clinging like a frightened animal,
hugging the tree, her eyes squeezed
tightly closed and her face white as
chalk beneath the soot. Tom suddenly
remembered Elenna had lost both
her parents in a fire, and his heart
clenched for his friend. But they had
to keep going.

"Elenna!" Tom croaked. His voice

hardly carried over the crackle of flames and she didn't move. "Elenna!" he tried again, louder. This time, she opened her eyes. "We have to lure Gorog to that acid pool. It isn't far," Tom told her. "He can't set fire to the water, but maybe that water can harm *him*!"

"But first we would have to get down," Elenna said, her eyes round with terror as she glanced at the flames below. "Tom... I don't know if I can do this."

"You can!" Tom told her. "You—" *BOOM!* The branch in Tom's burned hands bucked hard, forcing a cry of pain from between his teeth as he tightened his grip. Elenna yelped. Then a terrific creaking, popping sound filled the air and the tree began to lean. The movement seemed slow at first, almost graceful, but as the huge pine toppled, it quickly sped up, crashing through the branches of other trees. Twigs whipped at Tom, slicing his skin, and his stomach somersaulted.

"Jump!" he shouted, pushing off as hard as he could with both feet, hoping Elenna would do the same.

Tom threw himself into a roll as he hit the ground, then leapt to his feet to see the leaf litter around him burning. Elenna landed in a nearby drift of smouldering pine needles. Tom yanked her up just as the earth leapt and a deafening crash shook the forest. The tree they had jumped from had come down. Through the smoke and fire Tom saw the clearing with the fetid pool just ahead. His tunic had started to smoulder and flames licked around his boots. Elenna danced from foot to foot, slapping at the fire on her clothes. A furious howl rang out close behind them. *Gorog! It's now or never!* Tom thought. *I have to end this.*

"Elenna! The fire hasn't reached the

far side of the pool yet," Tom cried. "Run there and hide. Cover me! I won't be far behind you." Normally, Elenna would argue, and Tom saw her pause for a heartbeat before glancing at the flames and nodding. She took off at a terrified run.

Once his friend was out of sight, Tom put his hand to the red jewel in his belt, so he could communicate with the Beast. "Gorog!" Tom shouted into the smoke. "I'm over here! Come and fight, face to face! Or are you too afraid to meet a true flesh and blood Master of the Beasts?!" Tom heard a furious growl, and smiled. *He's coming... Now this plan had better work!*

ON DEADLY GROUND

As Tom reached the shore of the murky green pool he turned and drew his sword. His scorched palms screamed with agony, but he ignored the pain and, lifting the blade, fixed his eyes on the burning treeline ahead. Gorog burst through, snarling and slavering, his fur singed but his red eyes glowing brighter than ever. When they rested on Tom, they blazed with hatred. Gorog lowered his head, let out a furious growl, and lurched into a run. Tom held his ground, watching the massive Beast draw close, a blur of muscles and fangs and searing red eyes... Then, at the last moment, Tom dived sideways into a roll.

SPLASH! Tom sprang up to see Gorog sink chest deep in the acidic green water and clinging mud. With a roar, the varkule turned, thrashing and floundering, fumes bubbling up all around him. But then he caught sight of Tom and fell still,

his red eyes
narrowing.
Tom felt
their strange,
compelling
power. He
blinked and
shook his
head. But
the only

thing he could register apart from
the fixed gaze of the Beast was the
hideous pain in his burned hands.
If anything, the throbbing, searing
agony seemed worse than ever…he
could hardly catch his breath. *My
sword!* He realised the weapon was
getting hotter again. As hot as if

he'd pulled the blade straight from the forge. Tom staggered backwards, gasping, and slammed into a rotten trunk which splintered under his weight. But Gorog wasn't defeated yet. He couldn't let his weapon fall.

Tom lurched sideways and noticed that the tree he had hit was almost rotted through. The sight gave him an idea. Gripping his superheated weapon in both hands, ignoring the agony in his palms, he called on the strength of his golden breastplate and swung his sword with all his force, right into the blackened wound in the trunk. The blade bit through dead sinews, smashing the last of the wood. With a grating creak, the tree toppled down over the pool. *THUD!* It landed right on Gorog's massive head. Tom threw down his sword, panting with pain and relief.

But Gorog raged on, floundering in the noxious water, his red eyes blazing like furnaces, his powerful body propping up the trunk. The water foamed and bubbled around the Beast, and Tom could see clumps of the creature's fur floating in the vile soup. The stink of smoke from the burning forest mingled with the rank stench of the bog, and something worse still as the Beast's body started to dissolve. And yet Gorog would not stop thrashing. Tom gaped in horror at the sight. *Will he never give up?! Do I have to put him out of his misery?*

Calling again on the magical strength of his breastplate, Tom let out a roar and leapt high, landing with all his weight on the fallen tree. Gorog's head finally went under. The trunk juddered beneath Tom, but he kept his balance, willing the Beast to become still. Putrid yellow foam and brownish slime, as well as matted fur, billowed out from under the log, making the foul water murkier still. Finally, the tree trunk stopped shaking and began to sink. Tom leapt back to shore, to see the flames consuming the forest extinguished all at once, leaving blackened wood and smouldering ash smoking gently in the sudden quiet. Tom sank weakly to the ground, cradling his blistered hands to his chest.

Gorog's defeated!

Suddenly, the cackle of mocking laughter reached him through the trees. Weak with pain and exhaustion, Tom turned to see the pulsing light of Karadin's ring bobbing towards him through the singed trunks.

"Your Beast is gone," Tom said. "It's finished, Karadin."

The shadow man emerged, smiling broadly, and held his arm out towards the swamp. "No, boy – it has only just begun."

Tom watched, unable to fight the evil ghost, as the shimmering grey shadow of a varkule drifted up from the putrid pool and poured into Karadin's ring. The ring flared brighter for a moment. Then Karadin lowered his hand.

Tom heard a furious scream and turned his head just in time to see Elenna streak from the cover of a thorn bush, grab his abandoned sword from the ground and lunge towards Karadin. Without even looking her way, the evil ghost lifted his skeleton hand and snatched her up mid-leap, his bone fingers clamping tightly round her throat. Karadin smiled as Elenna dropped Tom's sword and kicked out at him, dangling in his grip. Tom tried to gather his strength. He staggered to his feet, but swayed and almost fell.

"See how my power has grown!" Karadin cried. "I will become stronger with each Beast that falls! Every battle you fight will bring me closer to my resurrection. All your efforts have been for nothing!"

"Stop!" another familiar voice shouted and Tom turned to see Loris appear nearby, his pale eyes earnest and his hands clasped, as if pleading with his brother. "Karadin, our time is long gone. Your chance to rule is behind us. Let the girl go, please!"

"Never!" Karadin hissed. "Our father stole my birthright. I will claim the throne of Avantia and I will rule over you all!"

Tom balled his hands into fists, wincing in pain, and staggered towards the evil ghost.

"Let her go!" Tom roared, aiming a punch at Karadin's jaw. But his hand swiped through empty air and Karadin howled with laughter, while Elenna kicked and choked. Tom gritted his teeth in frustration. But then he heard the howl of a wolf, and the pounding thud of hooves through the trees. His heart lifted. A moment later, Silver and Storm burst from the soot-blackened forest and both leapt towards the shadow man, Storm's hooves flashing as he reared and Silver's teeth bared in a snarl.

Karadin glanced towards the two animals. Seeing her captor distracted, Elenna grabbed Karadin's hand and started trying to prise his ring free. With a growl of fury, Karadin threw Elenna down, drew back his hand and slapped her hard across the face. Elenna fell to the ground, gasping for breath and holding her cheek.

"Remember! Fighting on will only make me stronger!" Karadin hissed, then turned and fled. Storm cantered after him, but pulled up once the spectre was out of sight, then lifted his head and let out a proud whinny.

Silver bounded to Elenna's side and started licking her face.

Rubbing at her bruised cheek, Elenna staggered up.

"Are you all right?" Tom asked his friend. "That was very brave of you."

"I'm...fine..." Elenna croaked.

"But your hands, Tom! They're burned!"

Loris drifted to Tom's side, his pale brow creased with worry.

"Whatever my brother says, you did well defeating the Beast," the ghost said. "But your burns are deep. You need help."

Tom heaved a ragged breath and drew himself up to stand tall. "I can heal my hands. But

the most important thing is to stop your brother waking another Beast. Where do you think he will go next?"

"It looks like he is heading north," Loris said.

Tom frowned. "There is no doubt that Karadin will awaken another Beast when he gets there," he said. "No. There will be time for rest and healing later. This Quest has only just begun and while there's blood in my veins, Karadin will not prevail! Let's go!"

THE END

CONGRATULATIONS, YOU HAVE COMPLETED THIS QUEST!

At the end of each chapter you were awarded a special gold coin.
The QUEST in this book was worth an amazing 8 coins.

Look at the Beast Quest totem picture opposite to see how far you've come in your journey to become

MASTER OF THE BEASTS.

The more books you read, the more coins you will collect!

Do you want your own
Beast Quest Totem?
1. Cut out and collect the coin below
2. Go to the Beast Quest website
3. Download and print out your totem
4. Add your coin to the totem

www.beastquest.co.uk

READ THE BOOKS, COLLECT THE COINS!
EARN COINS FOR EVERY CHAPTER YOU READ!

550+ COINS
MASTER OF THE BEASTS

550+
515
480
445

410 COINS
HERO

410
395
380
365

350

350 COINS
WARRIOR

320
290
260

230

230 COINS
KNIGHT

217
206
191

180

180 COINS
SQUIRE

146
112
78

44

44 COINS
PAGE

30
19

8

8 COINS
APPRENTICE

READ ALL THE BOOKS IN SERIES 27:
THE GHOST OF KARADIN!

GOROG
THE FIERY FIEND

DEVORA
THE DEATH FISH

RAPTEX
THE SKY HUNTER

GARGANTUA
THE SILENT ASSASSIN

Don't miss the next exciting Beast Quest book: DEVORA THE DEATH FISH!

Read on for a sneak peek...

THE HAND OF KARADIN

Tom bit his lip to keep from crying out as Elenna wrapped bandages around one of his injured hands. "If only I could find some willow bark to help heal the wound," Elenna said as she crouched beside the charred tree stump on which Tom slouched. She cast her eyes about doubtfully, and Tom followed her gaze. The forest was charred, and the bitter smell of smoke still lingered from the many fires Gorog had started.

Silver stood nearby, alert and watchful, his eyes glowing like twin moons against the smouldering remnants of the Forest of Fear. Beyond Elenna's wolf, Tom's stallion, Storm, pawed at the black earth, clearly as anxious to be off as Tom was. *We have to stop Karadin before he raises another Beast!*

Tom had been badly burned fighting Gorog, the deadly varkule-Beast raised by the Evil shadow ghost, Karadin. The healing powers of Epos's talon had stopped the blisters weeping, but Tom's palms were still red-raw and hurt as badly as ever.

"How does that feel?" Elenna asked, as she finished wrapping the second bandage.

"It's much better," he said through gritted teeth.

"Liar," said Elenna.

Tom managed a smile. "We need to get going."

As Tom spoke, a swirl of mist appeared at Elenna's shoulder, quickly resolving into a familiar, ghostly form. It was the spirit of Prince Loris, Karadin's younger brother. The two princes, sons of an ancient king called Mandor, had once shared the role of Master of the Beasts in Avantia. Karadin had returned from the dead after his skeleton hand was uncovered at King Hugo's Palace. Loris had appeared too, and was now helping Tom and Elenna on their Quest to stop Karadin taking Avantia's throne.

"My brother is already far ahead of us," Loris said, his pale, translucent face etched with worry. "But before you set off in pursuit, there are things you must know."

Tom nodded. "We had better be quick," he said.

Loris closed his eyes and drew his hands together. He stayed silent so long, Tom was about to protest – *This is no time for prayer!* – when suddenly, Elenna swayed and closed her eyes, and Tom's own eyelids became impossibly heavy. He couldn't keep them open... But, as they fell shut, instead of darkness, he was met with the clear, cold light of a winter's day. He could hear a high wind whistling, but his body felt numb. Even the pain of his burned hands had dulled to a distant throb.

"What is this?" Elenna asked, her voice sounding thin and far away.

"After my brother killed me, I followed him in ghost form," Loris said. "You are now seeing what I once did…"

Turning his attention to the scene before him, Tom saw a crescent of snow-capped mountains jutting into the sky, each peak as sharp and white as a wolf's tooth. Near the jagged summits, nestled on a rocky plateau, sat a small village of squat stone huts. The biggest building, a rectangular hall, stood in a courtyard at the heart of the village. Tom recognised the place.

"That's Colton!" he said. It was the highest town in Avantia, and barely seemed to have changed since Loris's time.

"Yes," Loris said. "Now watch."

As Tom looked closer, he saw a broad-shouldered knight dressed in full armour marching up a narrow path towards the mountain village, his dark cloak billowing behind him. In one hand, the warrior carried a broadsword, and in the other, a shield bearing the sigil of two crossed blades. A gleaming ring on his finger caught the sun, sending out rainbow sparks.

"Karadin!" Elenna said. Tom knew that she was right. The ghost they had encountered still wore the same snake-shaped ring on his skeleton hand – it was this that allowed him to raise Beasts.

"Once my father learned that my

brother had killed me," Loris went on, "he vowed to stop Karadin. However, he knew he could not defeat Karadin himself, so instead, he set a trap. My father sent his most feared warrior north to Colton, then made sure that stories of a Beast rampaging in the village reached my brother's ears. Karadin headed there immediately, expecting an easy victory. Instead, he found an ambush."

Right on cue, Tom's vision shifted, swooping in close to the village of Colton just as Karadin reached the empty market square and stopped before the town hall's heavy doors. He rapped on the wood with a fist.

"I come to defeat a Beast!" he bellowed.

The doors flew open, and a huge brute of a man stepped out. Clad in leather and chainmail, he stood a head taller than any warrior Tom had ever faced, and twice as broad. Bushy brows almost hid his fierce blue eyes and a red beard brushed his barrel chest. In one meaty hand, he brandished an axe few men could lift; in the other was an immense longsword. He smiled broadly, showing yellow stumps of teeth.

Read
DEVORA THE DEATH FISH
to find out what happens next!

Don't miss the thrilling new series from Adam Blade!

FROM THE CREATOR OF **BeastQuest**

ADAM BLADE

SPACE WARS

CURSE OF THE ROBO-DRAGON